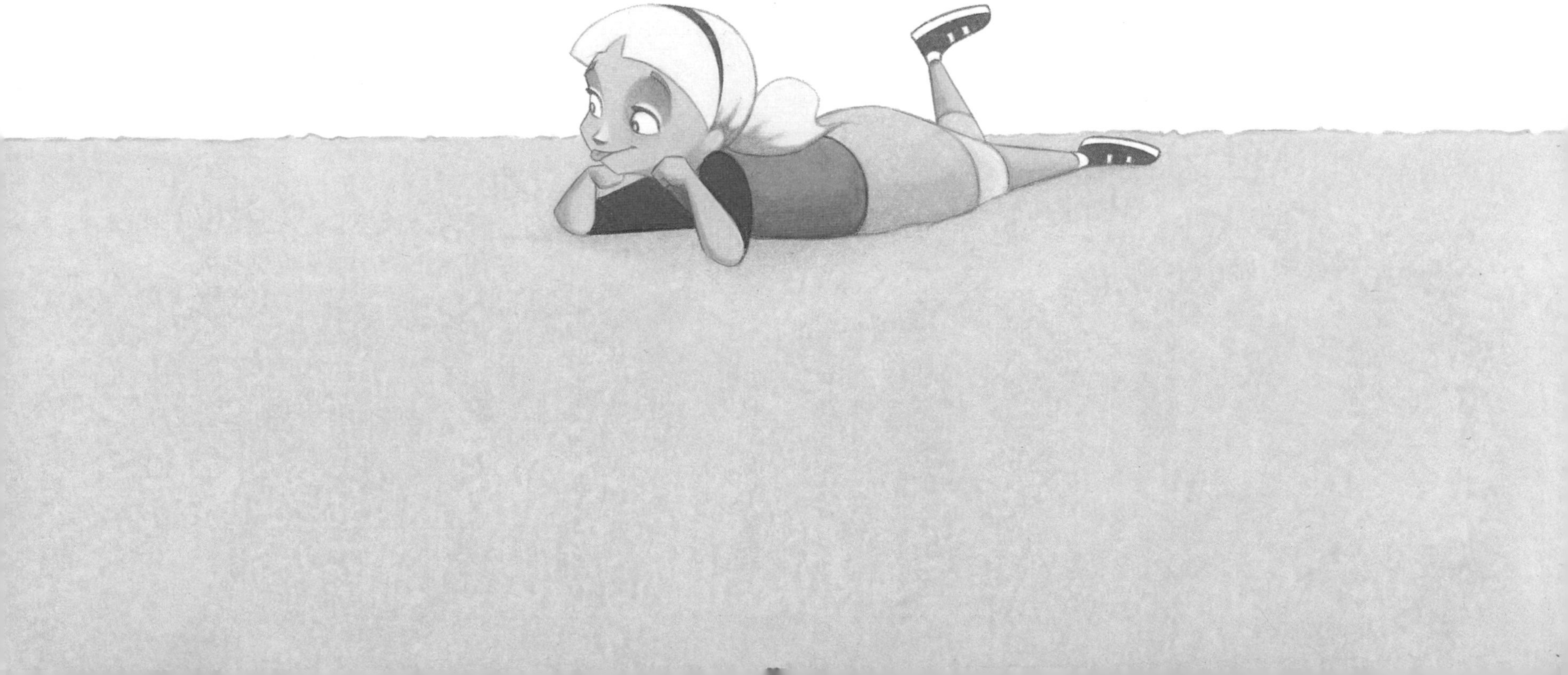

For my funny, fearless daughters, Sophie and Sasha
—J.M.

For Maria and Nicole
—M.I.

Copyright © 2017 by Jenna McCarthy
Jacket art and interior illustrations copyright © 2017 by Molly Idle

All rights reserved. Published in the United States by Random House Children's Books,
a division of Penguin Random House LLC, New York.

Random House and the colophon are registered trademarks of Penguin Random House LLC.

Visit us on the Web! randomhousekids.com

Educators and librarians, for a variety of teaching tools, visit us at RHTeachersLibrarians.com

Library of Congress Cataloging-in-Publication Data is available upon request.
ISBN 978-0-385-39086-6 (trade) — ISBN 978-0-375-97356-7 (lib. bdg.) — ISBN 978-0-385-39087-3 (ebook)
Book design by Nicole de las Heras
MANUFACTURED IN CHINA
10 9 8 7 6 5 4 3 2 1
First Edition
Random House Children's Books supports the First Amendment and celebrates the right to read.

POPPY LOUISE
Is NOT Afraid of Anything

Jenna McCarthy

illustrated by

Molly Idle

Random House  New York

Poppy Louise Littleton
is not afraid of anything.

When she sees a spider or a snake,
she scoops it right up.

All her imaginary friends
are monsters.

And when Poppy grows up, she wants to be a racecar driver.

The problem is, none of Poppy's friends are as brave as she is. At Fiona's house, Poppy wants to turn off all the lights and tell spooky stories.

But Fiona would rather put together a puzzle.

At the amusement park,
Poppy can't get anyone to go on
the big roller coaster with her.

She rides the little one and tries her best to smile.

"How do we get up on your roof?" she asks her friend Finn.
"We don't," Finn tells her.

"Rats," Poppy says.

Poppy's family is even worse.

"Let's go for a hike," Poppy suggests.

"It's nine o'clock at night!" her parents point out.

"There might be mountain lions out there," adds her sister, Petunia.

"I'll bring kitty treats!" Poppy offers.

People call Poppy the brave sister
and Petunia the careful sister.

Petunia prefers to think of herself as *wise*.

Poppy has been begging her
dad to throw her up in the air
since she learned how to talk.

"Higher!" she still cries
every time.
"That's high enough,"
her dad tells her.

He used to be way better at it.

Poppy's mom is always telling her not to pet strange dogs.
But no dogs seem strange to Poppy!

At Halloween, Poppy has the hardest time picking out a costume.

"Bumblebee?"

"Ballerina?"

"Butterfly?" her mom asks hopefully.

"Goblin!" Poppy finally decides.

At the zoo, Poppy's favorite animals are the alligators. She presses her face up against the glass and smiles at them. She loves it when the alligators smile back.

She'd stay there all day, but her family usually drags her away to see some boring birds.

Poppy thinks vampires are cute and mummies are funny.

And she's positive a tarantula would make a perfect pet.

"We could get you a goldfish," Poppy's parents offer.

"How about a shark?" Poppy asks.

"No!" they say.

"A bear?" Poppy tries.

"You really wouldn't be scared of a *bear*?" Petunia asks.

"Nope," Poppy insists.

Petunia isn't sure she believes her.

Petunia is determined to find something that scares Poppy.

She puts a lizard on Poppy's pillow.

Poppy names her Frankenstein
and knits her a tiny sweater.

Sometimes Petunia hides
under Poppy's bed and growls.
"I know that's you, Petunia,"
Poppy laughs.

"Grrrrrrrrr," Petunia replies.
Petunia doesn't give up easily.

But when Petunia needs something from the deepest, darkest part of the basement, she always calls Poppy.

Poppy, of course, is happy to help.

"Got it!" she announces proudly.

"Poppy Louise, you're a mess!" her mom moans.

"Yeah, but I got it!" Poppy says, beaming.

When Finn's remote-control
rocket gets stuck in a tree,
Poppy races straight to the top.

"Hooray!" Finn cheers.
Even Petunia is pleased.

Poppy stares at the ground.

It's very far away.

"Are you going to come back down?"
Finn finally asks.

"What are you waiting for?"
Petunia wants to know.

"I like it up here," Poppy insists.

"Mom made muffins," Petunia tries.

"I'm not hungry," Poppy says.

"But it's no fun without you down here," Petunia says.

Finn and Petunia fetch a ladder.

Poppy climbs down carefully.

"Do you want to do that again?" Finn asks.

"Maybe later," Poppy replies.

Petunia just smiles.